BIKER'S LITTLE FOR CHRISTMAS

ABDL MM Stuck Together MC Romance

Jerry Hastings
Michael Levi

Copyright © 2021 Jerry Hastings & Michael Levi

All rights reserved

The characters and events portrayed in this book are fictitious. Any similarity to real persons, living or dead, is coincidental and not intended by the author.

No part of this book may be reproduced, or stored in a retrieval system, or transmitted in any form or by any means, electronic, mechanical, photocopying, recording, or otherwise, without express written permission of the publisher.

ISBN: 9798777091710
Imprint: Independently published

1st edition

Cover design by: Jerry Hastings & Michael Levi

CONTENTS

CHAPTER 1

I shook my head, snow pieces flying out of my mouth. My eyes opened and closed, and I thought that I was seeing the face of a man right in front of me. Thinking that I was just imagining things, I ignored that thought and focused on how fucking cold it was around me. And not just around, but also inside of me. It was like it was winter in my cells, too.

Everything is going to be all right was what my friends said when they decided to bring me to this unimportant, ridiculous trip that wasn't going to add anything to my life. It wasn't going to make me richer, it wasn't going to bring me the boyfriend I was looking for, and it wasn't going to make me happy.

What it was making me do was think that I made the worst mistake of my life. My hands were digging into the snow and I couldn't make myself sit up. It was like something was pulling me down with force.

And when I reopened my eyes again, I realized I hadn't been wrong when I thought a man was standing in front of me. His hands on his knees, eyes icy-blue, it was like he was looking right into my soul. And yet, he wasn't what I was focusing on right now. Rather, it was the ridiculous amount of snow all around me. I wasn't rich, but I had paid a pretty penny on my clothes, and all this snow was destroying it.

"I thought you were dead," the man said, leaning in a little too close for comfort now. I had no idea what was going on in his mind, but he was making me feel extremely uncomfortable. And it wasn't just the fact that he was leaning in so close that I could smell him, but also that he was far too handsome for his own good.

Perfect beard, his blue eyes, skin overly smooth, hair cut short, and a bandana on his head. His leather coat made me wonder if he wasn't feeling cold. His jeans were skin tight and they were, again, making me wonder if he didn't mind the extremely low temperatures in this mountain.

At least his coat hid and protected his arms from the lower temperatures and the bone-freezing snow. He also had leather gloves that seemed to fit his hands perfectly. I couldn't see much of his skin, but the hint of something dark poking out of the collar of his white shirt told me that he had at least one tattoo on his body. For a moment, I wanted to ask him about it, but I chickened out on it.

I shouldn't be in this place and I shouldn't be interacting with this guy.

"Not yet," I said, pushing my body up and realizing that I couldn't - and I meant I really couldn't - sit up. The force that was pulling me down was still there. I also felt something a little warm and cold flowing down my arm, but didn't pay much attention to it.

The man smiled. "Looks like you like cracking jokes," he said, straightening up his back and dusting off his hands. What a jerk, I thought. I thought that he was going to offer me his hand to help me stand up.

Then, he turned back around to look at me. "You're hurt, and I've lost my motorcycle."

I widened my eyes. "I'm hurt? What are you talking about? I feel fine," I said, and I really did. Despite having my quirks, I wasn't the kind of person that lied, and especially not in a moment where there was just so much frigging snow everywhere. It was like it was trying to make me become a part of it.

"I'm going to help you stand up," he said, getting on my side and putting his arm around my waist. I wasn't going to moan about the fact that I was semi-hugging this hunk of a man, who was much taller than me, but I still found it inappropriate that he was touching me like this. He wasn't supposed to. I didn't tell him that he could and most importantly, I didn't even know his name.

"Hey, what are you doing?" I huffed and even though I was making it pretty clear that I wasn't liking this completely, he wasn't stopping. The man pulled me up strongly and confidently, smiling softly even though I could see that he was forcing himself to do that. When it came down to it, he wasn't the kind of man that smiled often.

If anything, he was making me feel like I was becoming a burden to him and that he was only doing this because he couldn't imagine himself not doing it. Feeling his hard muscles working, even if only briefly, made my dick hard in my pants. I was sporting a semi-boner, which was making me happy that I had heavy and thick pants on. The man couldn't see anything.

And he didn't retreat his arm like I thought he was going to. He was still supporting me against his weight, almost like he knew that if he let go of me now, I'd fall over on my ass.

"We need to find a safe place to hole up at. It's going to be snowing more soon, and I think that, this time, it's going to be a snowstorm," he warned, looking ahead and not into my eyes. For a moment, I was happy that his icy-cold blue eyes weren't staring at me. He made me feel so uncomfortable when he was doing that a few seconds ago.

"Wait, you still haven't explained anything to me about this," I grumbled and tried to move my body, realizing that a searing round of pain was shooting up through my arm. It was the first time that I was feeling it and it completely took me by surprise. Throwing my mouth open, I screamed and bellowed. It was the first time that I was feeling so much pain in my life.

And the man hugged me more tightly to his body without pressing his weight to my arm. If I wasn't surrounded by so much snow and he wasn't a complete stranger to me, I'd be able to pretend that he was my Daddy and was trying to help me feel better.

But I should be thankful that at least I had someone looking after me, even if he was a biker who didn't much care for me. I couldn't be sure about that, but I still was.

The heat of his body coupled with the beating of his heart helped calm me down. And after a while, I was already feeling better and even more uncomfortable than before. That was because I was probably pressing my boner to his legs. Unless my pants were thicker and heavier than I thought they were, he was feeling it.

If there was something I learned in my life, it was that people who looked straight probably were. And this huge, menacing, and imposing biker was as straight as they came. The piercing in his nose and his ears wasn't lying to me, after all. I was still a virgin and I wouldn't lie about that to him, but still... I supposed that nothing of that mattered right now.

"Sorry if I moved too suddenly. It's not going to happen again," he said, this time looking directly at me and making me feel at ease that he was here with me. He turned his head again and looked straight ahead. When his eyes went slightly wide, I knew he had found something important. "That looks like a cabin to me."

I turned my head to look at it, blinking twice until my eyes were better adjusted to what I was seeing. It was difficult seeing anything in this snow, and especially when it was covered partially by it, but the darker, smaller areas weren't lying to me. There was a cabin on this mountain and it was surrounded by a bunch of trees.

"I'm going to take you there. Think you can make it?" He asked and I just realized that if I was going to be spending some more time with him, that at least I needed to ask him something.

"What is your name? And why are you here?"

For a moment, I thought that he wasn't going to answer my questions, but then he said, "I'm Chris and, for now, you don't need to worry about the rest of my name. We need to be pragmatic about what's happening here. You're trapped with me in this mountain, hurt, and need someone to look after you. I can be that person, even though I can already see that you aren't thrilled about it. And trust me, the feeling is mutual."

A punch to the gut that was, but I was happy that he was laying it on the table and telling me what he was thinking. After all, despite knowing his name, Chris was still a stranger to me.

CHAPTER 2

Chris

What a mess. One moment I was riding through this mountain when, suddenly, I got a call and a semi-avalanche hit me. I lost control of my bike and couldn't even see where it was. Dammit, I thought. It was like everything was working against me, and I didn't know what to do about it. I was with this little guy, who wasn't a kind person, and certainly not the type of person that I should be trying to be friends with.

Everything was still a mess in my mind, I thought. One moment I was riding my motorcycle and the next I was next to him, snow piled up inside my mouth. I had no idea what happened to him, but the moment I realized that he was hurt and needed my help, I did exactly that.

Pushing open the door, I frowned at the moldy smell coming from inside the cabin. Looking inside it, I realized that it was the kind of place where I could spend some nights here, but the food was certainly going to be an issue. I was saying that because it was unlikely that whoever had lived here had left any food in the cupboards.

Even though I wasn't exactly keen on getting to know this guy, it looked like we were going to be spending some time here. He was groaning and wincing, showing me that he was feeling a lot of pain. As a Daddy, the first thing that came to my mind was that I needed to help him until he was feeling better.

I usually didn't use my phone as I thought it too distracting, but now that we were stranded in the mountains, I was kind of missing it.

Turning my head to him, I said, "You wouldn't happen to have your phone with you, would you?"

"If you would be so inclined as to put your hand in my pocket and check it out for yourself…" He said and I put my hand in his pocket right away. I poked around in it, but couldn't find anything.

"Nope, it looks like you also don't have your phone. I lost mine too," I said, not feeling like telling him that I didn't use my phone often. Right now, I didn't want to tell him much about me.

He groaned while I helped him sit on a chair. There was this chair, and another, and also a table in the kitchen. Or maybe I should be saying that the kitchen and the living room were in the same space. I wasn't going to say that the cabin was huge, because it wasn't, but it had enough space for two people to spend some days in it.

Not that I was thinking about spending any more time here than needed, but I was keeping that in mind.

After a moment, I went to his side to check his arm. He tried to move it away, but I said, "I just want to make sure that it's not as bad as it looks."

Mike groaned, moving his arm back so that I could see what had happened. Something had definitely made an incision in his skin, going from his elbow to his shoulder, and there was a lot of blood coming out of it. So much so that it was soaking his coat.

"So, how bad is it?" Mike asked, and I didn't like what this meant. I was going to have to kind of become a mountain man, get something around here to patch him up, and then hope that he wasn't going to get an infection. Even though we were two different people that didn't much like each other, I still wanted to make sure he was going to come out of this alive.

"It's not too bad," I lied. Sometimes, lying was better than telling the truth. "But I'm still going to find something to dress it."

Mike widened his eyes. "You mean that you don't have anything with you? I'm sorry, but I don't think you're going to find anything we can use in these woods."

I shook my head. "I might look like a biker, but I know my way around here. My dad used to live in a forest very similar to this one."

I stood up quickly and quietly, turning around when I felt something grabbing my hand. I was surprised and wasn't at the same time when I realized that it was him that was grabbing it. His hand was slightly trembling, like he was trying to tell me not to go.

"What are you doing?" I asked. Right now, it was everything I could ask him. Nothing was going to change the fact that we were both strangers to each other.

"Please don't leave me alone..." He responded and him saying that made me feel sorry for him. He wouldn't have said that if something terrible hadn't happened in his past. Now that he was making me think about it, I was asking myself what that was. But just like with everything I thought I needed to do here, I refrained from doing that.

I grabbed his hand and squeezed it gently. My hand was much bigger than his and now that was more obvious than before. My Daddy side was telling me that I couldn't walk out of this cabin without telling him he didn't have anything to worry about. Maybe there were bears on this mountain, but I doubted they were going to show up. At least, not while I was still around.

"I'm not going to be long. I'll look for something that can help you and then I'll be back quickly."

I let a moment pass, my Daddy side caressing his hand gently and showing that I was going to be here for him, no matter what happened. Even though I was a biker and most people thought I was cruel, that wasn't exactly true. When it came down to it, I was more caring than most people thought I was.

We didn't say anything else, and that silence calmed him a little. He slowly opened his hand and dropped his arm. He was looking down and looking cuter than before. I wasn't going to say that he was a Little, but something about him was showing me that he was. Deciding not to make this weird, I didn't say anything about that and just walked out of the cabin.

My feet were crunching in the snow as I walked around the cabin. I looked everywhere and eventually found something – or better yet, a couple of things that could help him with his wound. Some semi-wet leaves, resins, and natural ointments that I could use to patch it up. I was pretty sure they were going to bring a smile to his face.

I turned around and proceeded back to the cabin. The first thought that popped up in my mind was that I was going to find him right there seated on the chair and waiting for me. It wasn't like he could escape the cabin and that he would be fine. Mike needed me now even if he wasn't telling me that.

Taking another step and adjusting my eyes so that they could see better in the darkness, I wasn't too surprised when I found him with half of his body across the table, his eyes closed and a line of saliva running down on his chin. Mike fell asleep while I was looking for the stuff I was now holding in my hands.

After stepping into the cabin, I said, "Looks like someone should wake up."

I didn't want to make this any weirder than it was, and I was happy when he reopened his eyes and looked at me. Mike was so cute and it was such a shame that I couldn't tell him that. He deserved to know it even though he was being an ass to me. I mean, I was helping him with everything I could and he was still kind of not saying thanks to me.

He blinked twice, his eyes finding the stuff in my hands. "Oh, you found it." He frowned. "It still hurts a lot. I hope that these leaves and whatever else it is you're holding will make me feel better."

I squinted my left eye slightly. "What, you don't believe me?"

After a moment of silence, he said, "No, it's nothing like that. Anyway, just do what you gotta do."

I smiled. It wasn't something I did often, but with him, it felt easier to be doing it. I still had a boyfriend and for a very long moment in my life, I thought he was the right one, but I never felt at ease with him. Not like I was feeling with Mike.

CHAPTER 3

Mike

He was holding my arm, and his hand was making it look smaller than it really was. He was a more caring biker than I thought he was. Of all the things I thought were going to happen on my trip to this mountain, being stranded in a cabin with a biker wasn't on the list. I was still feeling kind of weird around him, but the way he was holding my arm was showing me that he cared about what he was doing. He wanted to see me well.

He looped the last leaf around my arm and, after spreading some resin on the leaf under it, he made it so I couldn't accidentally peel it off. I had no idea what kind of resin it was, but it was pretty strong. Much stronger than I thought it was going to be, especially for something that came from a tree.

He padded my arm gently and I said, "Thanks for doing this for me. I don't know what I'd be doing without you. As you can see, I'm not exactly cut out for this."

He was still on his knees when he asked, "So, what do you do for a living?"

I sighed, looking up at the ceiling of the cabin. I wasn't sure if I was ready to talk to him about my life.

Looking down and sighing again, I was hoping he wasn't getting the wrong impression from me. After talking to him a little and getting to know him, I felt like we could be a little more than what we were right now. After all, he was just a biker without a bike and not a killer. At least, I was hoping he wasn't.

"I finished high school last year, tried getting into MIT, but couldn't. The admission exam was too hard and I utterly blew it. I know I'm a failure."

Chris slightly squinted his eyes. It was like he was thinking what I said was bullshit. But it wasn't, and what I said to him was the truth.

"You know, I don't know you well yet, but I don't think you are a failure. The fact that you were trying to get into MIT proves that. I wouldn't even dream of doing something similar."

I was appreciative that he told me that, but he wasn't making me feel less of a failure than I was. It wasn't something I could correct about myself without some long therapy sessions. Now that I was stuck together with him, they were probably not going to happen. The only thing I had to be focusing on right now was getting out of here, after all.

"You may be right, but my father had some really high expectations for me and he wanted, most of all, to get me into MIT. It wasn't really what I wanted for my life, though."

I was now stepping into very dangerous territory. I wasn't going to say anything to this guy about the fact I liked diapers, onesies, and pretending that I was five all over again. If I did that, I was pretty sure he would think I was weird.

"We all grow out of our fathers eventually," he said, grabbing my hand even though he didn't need to. I knew why he was doing it. It was his way to tell me that whatever had happened in my life, I had his support. "And they all stop understanding who we are."

Sensing that I could change the direction our conversation was taking, I decided to ask, "So how did you become a biker?"

Chris blinked twice, showing me he didn't think I was going to be curious enough to ask him about that. He was still holding my hand, which was something I was thankful for. Even though I knew he couldn't be a Daddy, it was almost like he was showing me he was through the way he was holding my hand.

"I had a fall out with my father. We never really had a good relationship, to begin with. He just didn't approve of what I was doing with my life."

"And what were you doing with your life? I can't imagine that you just stumbled on the whole biker thing and decided to be one."

He shook his head, smiling gently again. Even though his teeth weren't overly white, they looked sharp and that, coupled with his lips, made me feel like kissing him. I had a thing for Caucasian, bully-looking guys that I could only find in men like him. I was hoping that that would never come out, but the more time passed, the righter it felt to tell him that - at least once.

"I'm actually gay, you know? My father didn't take well to that and thought I was confused about it. He even took me to a strip club and tried to show me how wrong I was about it, but it didn't work, obviously."

I widened my eyes. Of all the things I thought his response was going to be like, I never thought that he was going to tell me he was gay. I mean, a man as big as he was, with such a dominating and caring hand, gay? I couldn't even wrap my head around it.

And even though I shouldn't be feeling this way, I kinda was. I was feeling more connected to him because of the pain that was showing up in his eyes. He was remembering some very painful moments that happened in his past.

"I'm sorry about it. My father was actually very supportive of it when I told him about it, but then something else happened. And then, after that, he was never the same."

Chris widened his eyes. "You're gay too? I didn't think you were." He was looking straight into my eyes and, for a moment, it was like nothing was happening around us. It was like it was really just the two of us in a big, white space.

Suddenly, he moved his hand away and stood up. After moving his chair so that he was sitting closer to me, I decided to bring up again my first question, "And how did you become a biker? I can't imagine it was easy."

He took a deep breath. "No, it certainly wasn't easy. I couldn't say anything to them about my sexuality, so they all didn't know about it until I became an important member. I'm the treasurer and so they just can't kick me out, even though they are trying to." Chris chuckled. "But it looks like, given how long it's going to take for us to leave this mountain, they'll just think I'm dead and grant themselves their wish."

I widened my eyes. "Don't be so negative. It won't take that long."

Chris chuckled. "You know, we have to prepare for the worst. At least, it's good knowing that we've got something in common. Better than being with someone I can't relate to."

And if he was also a Daddy, we would have even more in common. Something in me was tempting me to ask him if he knew anything about ABDL, but then I thought it would be weird of me if I asked him that. It was better not to.

"That we do," I said, looking outside and realizing that the whiteness of the sky was being replaced by the darkness of the night. Without a phone and with no means of communication with the outside world, the only thing we could do was to talk. I wasn't the talkative kind of person, so I was already feeling anxious. And since I was known for having panic attacks, I was already putting my hand under the table. Chris was a very perceptive type of guy and he would notice there was something wrong with me if he saw it.

"And how is your arm feeling right now?" He asked, suddenly making me feel aware of it. I had almost forgotten about it. Now that I knew a little more about him, I was feeling that he was a little more palpable than I'd thought.

"Better than before. Thanks for patching it up."

Chris stood up and went over to the kitchen. "I guess we need to make dinner now." He turned his head to look at me again. "You probably think that I don't look it, but I'm actually a pretty good cook."

"I don't have another choice but to give you a chance. I hope you won't squander it," I joked and chuckled.

"I won't," he said after opening one of the cupboards and getting a pan that was still in it. It looked old and not like the kind of thing I'd like to use for dinner, but my stomach was rumbling and

I was hungry. I didn't have another choice.

CHAPTER 4

Chris

I shook my head, stepping back into the cabin. I was holding a hare over my right shoulder. Hunting the bunny had been easy. What was difficult was figuring out if Mike was going to like it. Knowing the kind of person he was, it was pretty obvious that this was the first time he was spending this much time in these woods.

Mike just wasn't used to being outside of the city.

I supposed that that didn't matter anyway. He was either going to eat it or stay hungry until tomorrow morning. I had a good feeling about that and I was thinking that we were probably going to have a good chance to leave here. And when we were out of this place, I was kind of thinking I was going to miss him.

Mike was splayed over the single bed in the kitchen-living room space. I had tucked him under several blankets, which thankfully, the cabin still had. It was kind of surprising that they were still there under the bed, but I didn't think much about it. When it came down to it, I was happy that we had something to keep him warm.

He told me that his wound was feeling better and I was happy about that. I mean, I knew that those resins and leaves were going to do the trick, but it was still good to have a confirmation.

Lying in the bed like that, it reaffirmed to me the thought that I was the only one standing between him and danger. His cheeks were slightly pinkish and his lips were red like the color of some berries outside. I didn't get them for him, of course. They were toxic.

I was happy he was getting some rest. He needed it after going through everything he went through today.

I dropped the hare on the table and then placed some logs on the stove. I was happy we still had some matches here. Using one of them, I lit a fire on the stove, put a pot on it, and then the hare and some water and other ingredients. Of course, I also prepared the hare the way it needed to be, with all necessary condiments. It was going to be delicious.

I sat down on the chair, realizing that I could've asked him what he liked. Maybe I could have gotten something else for Mike. He looked so cute, sleeping in the bed like that. After a moment, I realized there was something about it that was bugging me. I didn't want to wake him, but it would also be wrong of me not to do it.

Sighing, I stood up and went over to his bed. I was going to be calling it 'his bed' because I wasn't going to be sleeping in it. He hadn't covered his other arm – the one that wasn't hurt – and it was probably freezing right now. I had no idea how he was even sleeping when his whole body wasn't covered by the only blankets we had in the cabin.

Maybe I shouldn't even be this worried about him, but the truth was that I was.

I pulled up the blanket so that it was covering his exposed arm and my heart skipped a beat when he stirred. I thought he was going to wake up, but he didn't.

Well, now back to the kitchen part of this small room and prepare his dinner, I thought. When he woke up, he'd love it.

Losing track of time and focusing entirely on what I was doing, I finished cooking his dinner and was just turning around when I heard him stirring again. Looking at him, I saw him sitting up on his bed and stretching his arms over his head. He yawned and then looked at me, a smile on his face.

"Looks like someone slept well," I said, not feeling at all nervous if he was going to like my dinner or not. Everyone I made it for liked it, and I was pretty sure that, with him, it wasn't going to be much different.

His little nose sniffed the air. "That smells nice. What is it?"

"It's hare, cooked with some special ingredients."

"Are you going to tell me what those ingredients are?"

I smiled. "Maybe later."

Mike shook his head, pushing himself off the bed but then wincing when he felt another jolt of pain in his arm. He reached for it as he said, "It still hurts so much."

What he said made me feel a little worried about him. I didn't expect that his arm was going to be healed by now, but I still wanted to see him better. Not only did we have to get out of here as soon as possible, but I was also beginning to like him.

"Well, don't force it too much and I'm sure you're going to be fine. I promise you that we are going to get out of here before Christmas."

"Tomorrow is going to be Christmas Eve. I hope you're going to deliver on your promise."

I raised my arms slightly. "What? You don't believe a biker like me? You can ask everyone that knows me. They are all going to tell you that I never lie."

"I didn't say you were lying… It's just that with the snow falling outside, it's going to be difficult to get out of here before then. I may not be a mountain man and a biker like you, but I know a thing or two about the weather around here."

"You do?"

Mike smiled. "One of my hobbies is predicting the weather. I know it probably doesn't sound very believable to someone like you, but it's something I like doing."

"I really had no idea. You're full of surprises."

He waved his hand. "Now, getting back to the dinner you made for me. I hope you didn't put too much salt in it. I don't usually eat meat, but tonight I'm making an exception, and only because you are such a nice biker. You are nothing like the bikers I know."

When he sat down on the chair, I asked, "You know other

bikers, really? I didn't think you did. I mean, you're like the kind of person that just… wouldn't. And I don't mean that in a bad way, just that you probably only meet other students and your professors in college."

"Well, I'd appreciate it if you stopped making assumptions about me. I do know some other bikers, though not personally. Have you ever watched some of the documentaries the History Channel makes? They're very enlightening."

I gave him an uncomfortable smile. "What do you mean? I had no idea that the History Channel made documentaries on bikers like me."

He squinted his eyes. "I know what you guys do for a living. You kill and rob other people. That's the reason why I can't like you, no matter how nice you are trying to be right now."

I dropped the large spoon I had in my hand. Putting my hands on my waist, I said, "Mike, whatever it is that you saw on TV, I know it's not true."

"They interviewed real-life bikers. They spent days with them. I know I'm not making things up. You guys kill, rob, fool, and terrorize people that try to stand up to you. It's disgusting."

"You must be talking about the one-percenters," I said, letting a moment of silence settle in the cabin. "And if you know so much about us, then please tell me where my 1% patch is."

And having said that, I turned around slowly so that he didn't have any other reason to believe I was trying to fool him.

"So? Do you see anything?"

He shook his head, biting his lower lip. "No, but that doesn't mean anything. A biker is still a criminal as far as I'm concerned."

"Well, you said I needed to stop making assumptions about you and now I have to say that you need to stop doing the same." I let a moment of silence pass. "Are you at least going to eat what I made for you?"

"I'm not hungry anymore," he grumbled, turning around and walking out of the cabin. Stupefied by what I was seeing, I went after him, putting a hand on his shoulder. Mike whirled around, his eyes burning with such a rage I had never seen before. "Will you leave me alone?! I don't want to be near you anymore."

I thought about slapping his face or putting him in a timeout, only to remember that he wasn't my Little and I wasn't his Daddy.

Things were getting more and more complicated around here.

CHAPTER 5

I had no idea what I thought I was doing when I let him learn so much about me. He was a biker and, thus, more dangerous than all the animals and the snow around here. I supposed I should be happy that there wasn't enough snow yet to make it impossible to even get out of the cabin. That's what I was thinking right now anyway.

I couldn't be in the same space as him without feeling like punching his stomach. It didn't matter how much Chris tried showing me that he was a good person. I knew he wasn't.

He was a shitty person like all the other bikers. He wasn't going to fool me.

I looked over my shoulder and realized that he was coming out of the cabin too. I rolled my eyes and decided to continue onward on the path I was following. It sneaked through the trees and went somewhere in the mountain, but it wasn't a way out. I knew that because nothing here was easy.

I had no idea what I was doing, but I let him be nice to me. It wasn't going to happen again.

"Hey, Mike, wait up! Whatever it is you are worried about, I can explain. I'm different from the other bikers. I mean, how many gay bikers do you know?"

He was right about that. All the bikers I knew were womanizers and drunkards. The fact that he was gay didn't stop him from liking beers too much, though.

Either way, I wanted distance from him. Couldn't spend another minute near him without feeling disgusted that I let him help me. He could have done all sorts of terrible things while I was sleeping in that bed.

I thought that he was different, but then I remembered something that made me realize I was wrong about him.

"Mike!" I heard his voice echoing in the air and I didn't turn my head to see if he was coming in this direction. All I cared about was going somewhere safer.

Snowflakes were still coming down, piling up on my clothes and hair. My wound was a little better now, thanks to the dressing the biker put on it, but it was still hurting. My feet were feeling a little heavy, walking in the snow like this, but I knew I could push onward and at least… find a place that didn't suck too much.

I reached a clearing and stopped, looking behind me and hearing nothing that reminded me of Chris. Nothing that reminded me of his beard, blue eyes, and the way he looked at me. I should be safe here, for the time being. And going back to him? That thought wasn't even crossing my mind, thankfully.

I sat down by one of the large trees, resting my back on it. I wrapped my arms around my knees and looked at nowhere in particular. I wasn't paying attention to what was happening in my surroundings because my mind was focused on something else.

I didn't want to tell him this, but I didn't like him because something happened in my past which was impeding me from even being near him. Feeling like he didn't deserve to know anything about it, I decided to keep it to myself.

My lips were trembling. There was so much snow falling from the sky now it was like this was Frozen's world. It was piling up around me, the layers growing, trees swaying all around me, and I was feeling more lonely than ever before. It wasn't just my body that was cold, but also my heart.

It was now, more than ever before, that I needed someone to be near to.

I blinked once and felt my eyelids were too heavy. I blinked again, and nothing changed. They were still too heavy and I felt that I was going to pass out if I didn't move. But that was the thing – if I moved, I also felt like I would pass out. I made a mistake when I walked out of the cabin without a proper plan.

I blinked again and found out that I would rather be sleeping. What the hell - my mind tried to shout at me, but it was too late. My vision was already darkening and I was losing consciousness of what was happening. I was going to fall asleep in a mountain, and even though I was aware that couldn't lead to anything good, I was still letting it happen.

A moment later, I reopened my eyes and found a familiar, strange face above me. I was in the arms of a person, and that person looked like someone I knew well. A guy that once tried to become more than my boyfriend. He got pretty close, but it didn't happen because I was far too focused on my work. That's what I tried telling myself anyway, even though I knew why it really happened that way. It did so because I wasn't ready. I was too afraid of kissing him for the first time.

And because of that, since then, I hadn't kissed anyone yet.

My vision cleared up and I realized that the person carrying me was none other than Chris! Of course it had to be him. That was how things were like in this mountain. I didn't need to have lived here a long time to know that about it. There was no one else in this place. It was just him and me, and I was also pretty sure that all the people looking for us right now had no idea we were in this part of the mountain.

His arms were strong and comfortable. He was making me feel safe even though he shouldn't. I didn't know why he was making me feel conflicted about it. A biker like him once did something I could never forget and forgive…

"No, you're not allowed to do this," I mumbled, but that only earned me a smile from him. He was taking pleasure in what he was doing. He was getting me where he wanted me, and I couldn't see anything I could do to stop him.

"I don't think you should be speaking right now," he said, looking down at me with the eyes of a true Daddy, even though that couldn't be the case. No biker could be a Daddy and vice versa. He was playing with me now.

We stepped out of the trees and reached the clearing where the cabin was. I was still cradled in his arms and so weak after not eating anything that I just couldn't fight back. It was comfortable being in the arms of someone that could keep me safe, even if he was a despicable man. It didn't matter how much he showed me he was different from the other bikers. I wasn't going to believe him.

He continued toward the cabin and put me in the bed, pulling up the blankets. "And it looks like you really need to eat something. Food is a little cold, but I'm going to warm it up," he said, grabbing the bowl, dumping what was inside of it back in the pan, and staying in front of the stove without looking at me. It was like he was acting like all of this was normal to him.

Of course it all was. He'd been through so much worse. He robbed and killed people before. What the hell did I think he was going to be doing right now?

I was, however, kind of appreciating the fact that he was still being nice to me after everything I spewed on his face. He was still cooking that hare dinner and the smell was nice. I was going to admit that much to myself even though doing so just felt wrong.

"Look, you shouldn't be doing this. Let's just get out of here while we can."

"No, Mike," his voice was composed and controlled. He knew what he was doing and he wasn't ashamed of it. In fact, I'd say that he was in his natural habitat right now. Snow, trees, animals, hunting, and a person for him to take care of. What else could be better for him than this? "You shouldn't be talking right now."

It wasn't a thought I should be having right now. It was making me hate the guy more and more. And after going through periods where I was stressed so much, I didn't want to go through the same. Not here and not now. After all, this was supposed to be my vacation. I was supposed to be having fun with my friends, who were probably out there looking for me.

And how couldn't I be talking when I needed to? I needed to

express all my thoughts and show him that he couldn't keep me here. My wound was still healing, I was weak and he was cooking a delicious dinner for me, but it was still wrong to accept anything from a biker like him.

"I need to leave. I need to find my friends," I mumbled before falling asleep again and feeling like something was transporting me out of here. Finally, I was leaving this shit hole and everything was going to be a lot better when I woke up.

That was my hope at least.

CHAPTER 6

I had no idea why he feared bikers so much. I didn't even have the 1% patch and it had always been like that. Now that the other bikers of my gang knew about it, it was going to be like that for the rest of my life. Not to mention them kicking me out. I was pretty sure they already did that, thinking I was dead.

Dinner was ready and I was seated by the bed when Mike was reopening his eyes. Slowly but surely, he was looking around and remembering where he was. His eyes showed me that he was a little confused, but he was going back to being his normal self again, I was sure of it.

I was acting like his Daddy, saving him from the cold and giving him all the blankets we had in the cabin even though I didn't need to. When it came down to it, I couldn't pretend that I didn't like him. Mike had a good heart. He was just confused about bikers was all.

I was holding the bowl with his dinner in my hand. I made enough for us both, though tomorrow things were going to be a little more complicated.

Looking outside and seeing that the moon was already falling behind the trees, I could tell that 'tomorrow' was actually 'today'. I had no idea how much time he went without eating anything. As far as I knew, Mike was without food in his belly since coming here to the mountain. Now that I was this close to him and seeing his face better, I remembered I'd seen him before when we got to the base of the mountain. I hadn't paid much attention to him back then, though. At the time, he was nothing more than a stranger to me.

Now... I was wishing things had been a little different.

"I hope you're not thinking I'm going to change my mind about you just because you kind of saved me. I didn't need to be saved. I was happy where I was, and I was in the process of finding a way out of here."

I sighed slowly. Mike was making this so difficult.

"You need to eat this," I said, putting some of the soup in the spoon and taking it to his mouth. He didn't open it, though.

"I don't want anything from you. I know what you're doing - what the meaning of all this is."

"And what do you think I'm doing other than giving you food?"

"You're doing this to make me feel ashamed of myself and then to make me think you're a good guy. How many people did you kill and rob?"

"None. I'm a biker and I like bikes, but that's all it is. I know about the one-percenters, but they don't matter right now. I know they give us a bad rep, but... I don't know how else I can explain it to you."

He pursed his lips, throwing his head the other way. Crossing his arms, he was showing me that he wasn't going to budge. Not without a proper incentive, I thought.

A thought popped up in my mind. This whole time, I'd been acting like I was his Daddy. There were no diapers, pacis, onesies, and all the rest involved, but he was still being pretty immature. And the fact that, before, he was liking me showed me that there was a weak spot in him I could explore.

Which meant there was one thing I could do now.

"Look at me, Mike," I said, my voice firm. When he didn't look back, I reaffirmed, "Look at me, or else I'm going to leave."

And now he snapped his head back at me. His eyes were trembling. He was still the same Mike who grabbed my hand and begged me not to walk out of the cabin that time. He hadn't changed.

"Once the snow's melted a little, I'll help you find your friends, and then I'll disappear from your life, okay? You'll never see me again."

Mike just kept looking at me.

"You're not going to do that. You are lying to me," he said, his voice very low and showing me that he really didn't think I'd do good on my word.

I held out my pinky. "How about making a pinky promise? I'm sure you are familiar with it."

He looked at it with disbelief in his eyes. "I'm not going to do that and you're not going to keep fooling me. I'm better than this."

I didn't budge, keeping my pinky held out. I was staring into his eyes and the only thing going on in my mind right now was that I was going to keep insisting that he did this promise with me. It was important to me that he did.

Mike chuckled. "Now you're behaving like a child."

I curled up the corners of my lips. "See? I'm not the bad guy you are thinking I am."

"Perhaps not, and if it's going to make you feel better, then at least I can do this," he said, lifting his hand and connecting his pinky with mine.

"There. That wasn't so hard," I joked, lifting the hand that was holding the spoon again. "And now, I'm going to insist that you eat this again. It's not going to be that hard."

He lowered his arms. "All right, I'm going to let you have this victory as well, but it doesn't mean that I'm beginning to like you."

"Of course not. It's not my intention to make you like me," I said, approaching the spoon to his mouth and finding it surprising that he was opening it. I really thought that he was going to be much more asshole-y right now. I was glad that I was changing his mind, even if only a little.

"We'll see about that," he said, swallowing the soup and munching the pieces of meat in it.

And then I asked, "So, do you like it?"

"It's not bad at all…"

Mike saying that made me feel better about everything going on between us. We went through so much, after all, and we needed this moment where we didn't feel like we were fighting against each other.

Lifting my hand again, I put the spoon in his mouth and he ate everything that was in it. Swallowing it and munching the pieces of meat, I could tell he was enjoying the taste of the food.

When he finished swallowing it again, I asked, "So, are you going to tell me the real reason why you don't like bikers? I know that we have our problems, but we aren't that bad."

"Could we just focus on the dinner? I'd appreciate it if we did."

"Of course."

Even though I was a little disappointed that all he was going to do now was eat, I was feeling better that he wasn't going to be hungry. The soup I made was full of pieces of hare meat and some other things that could satiate anyone's hunger.

Minutes later, I looked down at the bowl in my hands and noticed that it was empty. The spoon scratched against the surface, collecting nothing more than the rest that was on it. Mike blinked twice, and I could see the hunger in his eyes. He really liked the soup way more than he showed me he did.

"This is what's left. Make the most of it," I said with a joking tone.

"I still don't like you at all, but your soup is really good," Mike said, opening his mouth again and closing it around the spoon. Munching the meat pieces and then swallowing everything, he curved the corner of his lips before realizing he shouldn't do that. And he knew he shouldn't because he didn't want to make me feel like he was liking me.

I shook my head and stood up. Even though he was going to think I didn't win this little confrontation we had, I knew I did. When it came down to it, he wasn't a bad person.

He gave me a chance and now it was time for me to seize it.

CHAPTER 7

I was shivering, the bedsheets not feeling warm enough for me. Not even the blankets were warm enough. I wanted to have the heat of a person making me feel warmer now. But the only available person was lying on the floor, sleeping without the blankets. He gave them all to me even though he didn't need to.

I had no idea why this biker was being so nice to me.

And I also had no idea why someone as old as me still didn't have a boyfriend yet.

Well, I actually knew why. I just didn't want to think about the reason right now.

I shook my head. There was no point thinking about those things tonight. What I needed to focus on was getting some sleep. I fell asleep sometimes when I was in the cabin and when I was outside, but I didn't really get any rest. I needed to sleep at least eight hours nonstop to feel rested.

But there was something that was stopping me from feeling tired. And I meant feeling tired to the point of feeling like I was going to fall asleep.

I hated even thinking about it, but his snoring was making me feel like ripping a hole in his neck. It was almost like we were in a very closed room where no sound could escape. Chris was snoring like he was a machine made for that.

It wouldn't all be so bad if he wasn't sleeping on the floor. He was making me feel guilty. I mean, he was much older and I knew that his body needed more heat than I did. After all, my clothes were much thicker and heavier than his. My clothes were made for this kind of winter and cold.

And yet I could do nothing about that. He was sleeping on the floor, and that had been his choice. After he fed me that delicious soup, I was beginning to see he was a little different than the bikers I knew. He was more caring and did something for me that a biker I knew never would. He cared for me and made sure I was okay and well-fed.

But my body was still shivering. It didn't matter how many blankets I had over my body – I still felt like I was covered by the snow.

His snoring stopped and I heard him moving. Oh shit, I thought. He was going to hear me shivering and was going to be talking to me. There were moments when I was shy and this was one of them. If there was something I hated with my guts, it was when everything was silent and I could only focus on a very particular noise that drove me nuts. It was like something was poking my brain.

"Mike? Are you feeling okay? It's almost like you're still feeling too cold."

For a moment, I said nothing. Like I thought before, I didn't want to talk to anyone right now.

"Mike? Trying to fool me into thinking that you are sleeping isn't going to help. I said it before and I'm going to say it again - whenever you need my help, I'm always going to be with you."

"I'm not cold. It's just that-"

"You shouldn't make me feel like I'm repeating myself. I know you're cold and I want to help."

I didn't say anything, but I moved my hand down and found his shoulder. The bed where I was sleeping wasn't too tall, and he was lying on the floor right next to me.

I brushed my hand over his shoulder. And in that brief moment, he didn't say anything, but then I heard him standing up and tucking himself under the blankets. It was a single bed, but I felt that I was so small we could both sleep together in it. Not that I was feeling we were actually going to - it was just that we were doing this because we wanted to get through the night without feeling like we were going to die.

Chris didn't wrap his arms around me or do anything that I would think was stupid. He was just lying next to me, and it was nice. Having his body so near mine was indeed already making me feel better. I was already feeling warmer and I could see myself sleeping through the night with us in the same bed.

"How are you feeling now? Better already?" He asked, and I started to imagine what it would be like if we started to make out right now. I knew that the chances of that happening were slim to none, but my mind couldn't help but be imaginative right now.

"Better, yeah. I like that you are also not making this weird. It's just two gay guys lying in the same bed, right?" I said, seeing his eyes right in front of me. This time, I could smell his smell and it was a little different than that other time I smelled it. It was rawer, stronger, more masculine, and it was also really turning me on.

"Good. I feel better too. I was so cold on the floor."

"I had no idea what you were thinking when you decided that sleeping on the floor was a good idea. I mean, as you can see, the bed is big enough for the both of us."

"After we said that we were both gay, I didn't want you to think I was going to take advantage of you. It doesn't matter that you think I'm a bad guy just because I'm a biker. I'm different from most other bikers, and I don't say that lightly."

"I can see that you are, but it's still so difficult for me to connect to anyone."

"Why is that? Is there something you want to tell me?"

"Nothing out of the ordinary. I'm just shy and very antisocial. I've always been like that."

A moment of silence ensued, and I didn't know what else to say. He was looking into my eyes through the darkness in the room and I was still feeling the heat of his body pulsing to me. I almost wished we could be holding our hands so that I felt like I really had a friend right now.

"You know, Mike, I want to be someone you can rely on, but I can't do that if you don't open up to me. I promise you I won't bite."

I took a deep breath.

"Thanks, but I don't think it can happen that way."

"Why not?" He asked, his hand moving under the blankets suspiciously. He was making me think things I wanted to keep hidden from him. The truth was that I was aroused by him. I wasn't going to deny that he was perfect, looking like a bully that I wanted to be in the arms of. I kinda was when he rescued me, but that was a long time ago – or at least, it felt like it happened years ago. I felt like I had been living with him for more than the one or two days we had been together.

"You have no idea how hard it is for me to open up to people. Last time that happened, or I allowed it to happen, I was hurt."

"Well, it's the middle of the night and it's only getting darker outside. I'm not saying that you have to tell me anything, but I'm the only person you can talk to right now..."

I took a deep breath in and thought about it. The worst thing that could happen if I opened up to him was him telling his friends about it, and they wouldn't be able to do anything. After all, Chris didn't even know my full name.

"There is something about me you need to know before this gets any weirder." And as I said that, I felt my heart racing. I had no idea if I was doing the right thing or not, but it was happening either way.

I saw his head perking up. "Please, tell me everything. I'm all ears."

I chuckled. "You know, the last thing I thought I was going to find here in this mountain was a man like you. I hate you, but I can't deny that you are caring. You're showing that you like me."

"That's me," he said, putting his hand on my thigh and even though I knew he was crossing a line, I did nothing to stop it. I liked it. It was the first time that I was letting a man do what he was doing with me. "And so, are you going to tell me what it is that is eating up your mind? I'm dying to know."

I took another deep breath. This was a breakthrough in my relationship life and I knew it.

CHAPTER 8

Chris

My heart was in my throat and it was the first time that this was happening. I wasn't the kind of person that felt nervous about anything. I was connecting to this guy who was looking more and more like a broken Little. His life was a mess and he needed someone to sort it out.

"Do you know anything about ABDL?" He asked, moving his hand so that it was on mine. I never thought that he was going to be so accepting of what I was doing. I thought he was going to hate me for this. After all, I didn't want him to think I was taking advantage of the situation.

My heart sped up again. ABDL? Really? I knew all about it and even though he didn't say anything else, he was already making me think that, indeed, he was a Little. "Mike... It's like one of my dreams is becoming real."

"I'm going to take it that you know what I'm talking about. I'm saying that because most people don't know anything about it and when I do try to explain it, they think I'm a weirdo."

I lifted my hand and settled it on his cheek. "I know. It's always like that when I try to say that I'm a Daddy."

Mike chuckled. "Now you're making me blush that this whole time I've been with a Daddy. I mean, I thought you were just a biker like all the others. Are you telling me that they wanted to kick you out of the club because of that?"

I chuckled this time. "Something like that. They really, really thought I was going crazy or that I was pulling their leg."

A moment of silence settled in and I wanted to know what Mike was thinking. I wanted to get inside his head and learn everything about his past, even though I was aware that doing so wouldn't be fun. The fun thing now was digging out everything that happened in his past.

He was so warm I just wanted to be much closer to him than I was now. I wanted to be pressing my body against Mike's and telling him what a special person he was. Our relationship was getting better by leaps and bounds, but I still wanted to take things slow.

"Now that the truth is out, I was thinking maybe…" He trailed off, his hand slightly squeezing mine. My dick was getting harder at the thought of us doing something more than surviving here, especially because Christmas was nearing and I didn't want to spend it without doing something special.

"Don't keep me hanging here. Tell me what it is you're thinking."

Mike looked outside. "Looks like there isn't going to be a way for us to get off the mountain, so we might as well make the most of this."

"I like the change in your attitude." And as I said that, I pushed myself closer to him. I was crossing a line and I didn't care. It was cold and Mike was the only thing keeping me warm right now. "And so, what is it that you are thinking about doing with me right now?"

"Well, maybe not right now… I just wanted to be in your arms for a little while. I promise you that it won't be long."

I was looking into his eyes and I could see that they were shining gently under the moonlight. A crack in the wall behind me was letting some moonlight rays fall on his face. He was now looking cuter than ever before.

And even though I wasn't going to say this to Mike, I was already fantasizing about it. I wanted to kiss him. I wanted to make this something more than just the two of us holding each other close like this.

"I think that's perfect," I murmured, putting an arm around him and then pushing myself until I was pressing my body against his. He was so warm he was making it feel like there was no snowstorm outside. It was strong and raging, making the trees shake violently. So many snowflakes were flying and falling outside that I knew tomorrow morning the front of the cabin was going to be covered by it. And not just the front, but also all the other sides. Going outside was going to be almost impossible.

"You really are much kinder than I thought you were, especially for a biker." And as he said that, I noticed his eyes moving up and down. He was analyzing something he was seeing on my body, and it was making me curious about it too.

"So, are you going to tell me what it is that has gotten you so interested?" I asked, moving my hand up and down over his thigh.

"I see that you have all kinds of tattoos on your body, and I also noticed you have a pretty big one on your chest. I'm kind of curious about it."

Mike didn't hesitate before putting his finger on my chest, even though he didn't need to. I was feeling his finger pressing against it, and that was really making me feel more connected to him. I wished I could call him my boyfriend.

I knew which tattoo he was talking about. "Ahh, you mean this one. Do you really want to hear the story behind it? It's a long one and by the time I'm finished with it, you are going to be sleeping."

Mike opened a smile. His teeth were so pretty and his lips even more so. I didn't just want to be kissing him right now, but also to be making love with him. "I think I want that, especially because otherwise I won't be able to fall asleep."

"Alright then, so you remember that I told you about my father? Well, I decided to get this tattoo when he didn't want me to keep living with him, and that was also when I decided I needed to move out."

"I'm guessing that was when you found your bike club?"

"That's right, and that was when I went through the whole initiation process. It was kind of rough."

"Let me guess, they made you fuck girls to get into it?"

I chuckled. "Something like that, though I convinced her I wasn't going to do anything with her that night, and she was kind enough not to tell them about it."

"Must have really sucked. My father was understanding and didn't ask me to do anything similar."

"You grew up in an environment much different than mine," I said, my hand feeling his thigh through his pants. I was just happy that he was warm and comfortable. Mike stopped shivering.

"I did, and now I'm feeling a little guilty about it. I should have told my father years before I did that I'm gay. It would all have been better. I spent so much time thinking he was going to hate me."

His hand looked for mine and he grabbed it. It was small and comforting, and everything I thought it was going to be. I was happy I was here to make him feel better about all this.

"What made you think he wasn't going to like you?" I asked, realizing that I was diving deeper into his life. I wanted to because I wanted to find out everything about him. He was still just a stranger to me, but there were plenty of things about him I wanted to know about.

"He was very religious and wasn't like the kind of person I found approachable. There were so many times where he made it pretty clear he didn't like gays, even though we are all supposed to be God's people."

I caressed his hand slightly. "I'm really sorry about that. My father was a piece of shit, but at least he wasn't religious. That's something about him I'm thankful for. I have no idea what I would've done if he had been."

Mike widened his eyes. "You mean that he is dead?" He asked, his hand now squeezing mine gently. The connection I was feeling to him was growing stronger, and it was everything I wanted right now.

My cock wasn't even hard anymore. This was a very romantic and endearing moment that was really bringing out the best he had. We just wanted to keep ourselves warm during this harsh snowstorm going on outside. So much snow was falling and painting the landscape that it was already a couple of feet tall outside, some trees even falling over. Going outside tomorrow morning was going to be a pain in the ass, but I was still looking forward to it.

Since it was going to be Christmas, I wanted to do something special for this special Little I was getting to know.

CHAPTER 9

I woke up, my arm looking for him. But all I found was the emptiness that was on the side of his bed. And I was saying that it was his bed just like I thought that this was his cabin. And this forest? It was also his.

Turning my head left, all I could see outside the cabin was snow and more snow. That and also the trees that weren't shaking violently anymore. They were still swaying in the wind, but the latter wasn't as strong as it had been last night.

Without Chris hugging me, I was cold. Colder than I had ever been, even though we had an amazing night that was forever going to remain in my mind. I just found out that he was a Daddy, on top of being a biker. It was a weird combination that felt right at the same time.

I sat up on the bed and I turned my head right when I heard a noise coming from there. I blinked twice, feeling confused. I couldn't see anything coming from there. It was like the place was empty and filled with something at the same time. And that something was Chris's presence. He seemed to be everywhere in the cabin.

After going through all my college stuff and the stress in my adult life, I wanted to pretend that I was five years old again. But doing that was difficult when we were in the mountains and I didn't have anything I needed for that. Certainly not my onesies, diapers, sippy cups, and pretty much everything else that came with that world.

But there was something in the cabin that was filling the void, and it was Chris. I was still groggy and waking up, so it was no surprise that he was actually here with me, but wasn't perceived by my mind when I first looked in that direction.

He was holding a bowl in his hand and also something that he was using to smash whatever was inside of it. I had no idea what he was doing, but it looked edible. He was taking it to me and I was already salivating at the thought of having breakfast this morning. I was starving, after all.

He probably heard the rumbling of my stomach, for he smiled when he looked at me. "Good morning, sunshine. I hope you're having a fantastic day."

"Yes, Daddy!" I said, throwing my arms out and waiting until he was hugging me. He put the bowl and what appeared to be some kind of special spoon aside, wrapping his arms around me. As soon as he was hugging me, I felt the comfort and the heat of his body. It was everything I needed this morning, other than some food in my belly.

We ended the hug and he rubbed my hair gently. Before we fell asleep, we decided that we should roleplay as Daddy and Little for the time being. It was going to be my way to cope with everything that was happening in my life. It was going to be perfect for me to deal with the fact that I wasn't going to be heading back to the city anytime soon.

"It's early in the morning and I think you should have some breakfast before we go out."

And as he said that, I was already missing the heat of his body. It was the only thing that could really keep me warm right now.

"What did you make for me?" I asked, eager to look into the bowl, even though he was standing between me and it.

"I don't really have a name for it, but it's something special I made with some stuff I found in the forest. It's a little vegetarian, but I'm pretty sure you're going to like it."

"But Daddy, I have the most amazing thing to tell you!" I exclaimed, fisting a hand and throwing it up over my head. I was even changing my voice so that it was a little more high-pitched than normal. I wasn't normal, boring, and adult Mike right now. I was five years old again.

Daddy sat on the bed, picking me up and putting me on his lap. Looking into my eyes, he said, "Tell me what it is, then. I want to know everything."

That was one thing about my Daddy - my biker Daddy, I corrected myself – I loved a lot. He was always eager to hear what I had to say.

"I think I feel a little shy telling you this." And when I said that, I tried to hide my face from him. Even though I was a Little now, I was never going to change completely. I was always going to be shy in certain moments.

But he put his hand on my chin and turned my head so that he was looking straight into my eyes again. That was his way of telling me I didn't need to worry about anything. He was always going to give me all the support I needed.

"When I'm around, you don't need to feel shy about anything."

"You're right, but…"

He put his finger on my lips, closing them. "Like I said, no need to feel shy. It's all going to be okay."

I wished I could kiss him now, even though I knew I shouldn't. I liked to keep things separate. When I was a Little, there was never anything sexual in it. When I was his boyfriend, things were wildly different.

"I actually don't mind it when I don't have to eat meat. I've always been a little vegetarian. I only eat meat when I feel like people are putting pressure on me to eat it."

I thought that his reaction was going to be harsher, but he just shook his head and chuckled. "Really? That's what was making you feel so shy right now? It's actually perfect that you are a little more vegetarian than most people. We are in a forest and thus we have loads of options to fill your little belly."

As soon as he finished saying that, he shot his hands to my belly and started to rub it, making me feel tickles all over it. I was squirming and laughing as he continued that, and it looked like it wasn't going to end anytime soon.

When his hands finally stopped rubbing my belly, I was panting and sweating a little. I never thought that it was possible to sweat when the temperatures were so low, but here he was, proving me wrong again. What I was feeling guilty about right now, was that I never gave him a proper chance when I met him. We were still very early in our relationship, so I still had a lot of time to make things right.

"Daddy, that was amazing! I still feel like you are rubbing my belly."

I was still seated on his lap and I could feel the heat of his body pulsing around me. I could even hear the beating of his heart like it was mine.

"Well, I'll always tickle you when I feel like it." He picked up the bowl that was on a table by the bed. "And now that we finished talking about that, it's time to try feeding you. We are going to do something special outside that is going to require you to have a full belly."

"What thing?" I asked, hoping that he was thinking the same I was. Setting up a Christmas tree outside, decorating it with whatever we had here, and all kinds of other things. Now that I was thinking about it, we hadn't fully explored this cabin yet. We hadn't checked out if there was anything under it.

Perhaps there was a surprise there...

"Something that I'm going to tell you when you've finished eating this," he said. I looked down at the bowl and realized that it looked like some kind of porridge. I wasn't going to ask what it was made of, but the smell was pretty delicious. It was making my stomach rumble even though I had no idea what was there. But Daddy had my full confidence in him, and so I didn't need to worry about anything.

He scooped up some porridge with the spoon and guided it into my mouth. I closed my lips around it and started to chew it. The taste was delicious and warmed my heart. Daddy must have heated it using the stove and some logs that were still lying around in the cabin. He was so handy and resourceful. I wouldn't have survived the first hour here without his help.

And I was so friggin happy he was feeding me this delicious, vegetarian porridge!

CHAPTER 10

Chris

I never thought that things were going to happen so easily with him. He decided to become my Little and boyfriend even though, in his past, he was never open to relationships. I was so happy that he decided to change his mind about it.

And now, finally taking him out of the cabin, we were enjoying the scenery around us. I was holding his hand while he was turning his head from left to right and vice versa as he took in everything he was seeing. The piles of snow, trees swaying gently in the wind, and some animals scurrying between the trees and shrubs - it was perfect.

And his hand was as soft as ever.

I looked down, noting again that I was much taller than him. He was so happy that he was swinging his arms as he strolled around with me in the forest. There was still so much snow that the paths down the mountain were entirely covered by it, and we had no choice but to keep living here. It was great, actually. I was learning a lot about him and who I was.

His cheeks were slightly rosy, and it was clear that he wasn't feeling cold anymore. The hand I was holding was telling me so. I wouldn't say that he was already my boyfriend, but he was kind of becoming that as time passed.

He stopped in his tracks all of a sudden, shooting his arm up and pointing with his finger toward something in the distance.

"Look, Daddy! A deer."

I turned my head to look at it, not surprised that I was seeing it too. I had seen it much before he did. I'd always been kind of like a hunter, so my eyes were trained to spot animals like that deer. And when the deer finally saw us, it whirled around and ran off, kicking up chunks of snow behind it.

I rubbed his head vigorously. "You lifted your arm so fast you scared it."

Mike pouted. "I didn't mean to do that. I was just happy that I was finally seeing a deer for the first time in my life."

"Well, my sunshine," I said, realizing that sunshine was one of the things I most missed right now. That and being able to lounge on the beach, sipping from my coconut. That was something I was planning on doing with Mike when we were out of here. "You're going to get a lot of other chances to see more deers."

"Really, Daddy? I'm so excited!" He said, suddenly beginning to run around me as he made little jumps on the snow. I was happy that he was so excited about seeing the deers, but we had come here for something else. It was Christmas and I didn't have anything to give to him as a gift. That was embarrassing and I needed to do something about it. "And I also can't wait to be decorating a Christmas tree with you."

I squeezed his hand gently again. "We are going to do much more than that."

We turned to the right, going through some trees while we trudged in the snow that just seemed to be clinging to our feet. Walking was so difficult especially when we didn't have snow boots and the proper equipment to get around. But the only thing that mattered the most was the fact that he had a big, beautiful smile on his face.

Taking another step after we got out of the trees, I spotted something in the distance that seemed as if it was made just for us. It was like someone left it there just so that we could use it.

I lifted my arm and pointed at it with my finger. "Do you see that? What do you think about snowboarding a little right now?"

Mikey was already leaping around me in the snow. He was giggling and so happy that he just couldn't hide the smile on his face. "Of course I want to, Daddy! I'm so excited!"

Everything that came out of his mouth was exaggerated and coated with his happiness. Likewise, his happiness was rubbing off on me and I was just as excited to snowboard with him.

We walked over to the snowboard equipment that was by one of the large trees and we put the boards on the ground. Other than that and the goggles, we didn't have any other equipment to do this properly. We weren't going to snowboard properly, but that was okay. When we were out of here and we had money and everything else, we were going to do everything we wanted.

He slipped his feet into the snowboarding boots and his body wobbled as he started to lose his balance. I put an arm around his waist and held him close to me, rebalancing him.

"Whoa there, sunshine. You gotta be more careful when putting your feet in the boots. You'll fall otherwise."

"But I'm just so excited, Daddy! It's the first time I'm snowboarding."

And even though he didn't say it, I was pretty sure he was thinking I was the perfect person he was doing this with. After all, I had the experience and everything else I needed.

Looking to the right, I spotted a nice, gentle slope that didn't go too far down the bottom. Keeping a hand on his back as I led him to the top of the slope, I could feel that his legs were shaking.

Putting my other hand on his back and lifting my left hand so that it was sitting on his shoulder, I looked down to the bottom of the slope, seeing what it was that he was seeing. I could feel his pulse beating against my face, and I could tell that his heart was racing.

"It's pretty scary, but I'm going to be holding your hand the whole way down. You don't need to worry about anything."

"But I'm a little scared. It feels like I'm going to fall off a huge mountain."

I lowered my arm and grabbed his hand – the one that was gripping the leash. He was gripping it so tightly that his knuckles were white. "It's just a small slope. I'm going to be with you the whole way down, like I said."

It was going to be easy for me to do that because we didn't have another pair of boards. He was the only one that was actually going to snowboard down the slope. It didn't mean that his hands were going to stop shaking, but it was better than him doing this alone.

He gritted his teeth and fixed his gaze on the bottom of the slope. Not only was it gentle and followed a small angle, but it also didn't have any trees.

"And you know the other thing we are going to do after I teach you how to snowboard?"

When I asked him that, he opened a smile as his hands stopped shaking slightly.

"The Christmas tree," he said, and I kissed his right cheek for good luck.

I studied his eyes for a second and realized that he was feeling ready. I took a step forward as I pushed him down the slope gently. He was sliding down, and his knees were still wobbling. I could see that it was going to take him a long time until he was used to snowboarding.

A minute later, he was reaching the bottom of the slope. He jumped out of the boots and threw himself at me, hugging me tightly. "We did! I did it! I'm so fucking happy!" He shouted over and over, and I could feel how genuine his words were.

I whirled around with him, hoisting him in my arms while he cradled his head in the crook of my neck.

Moving him backward, I asked, "Ready to do this again?"

"Yes, Daddy!" He answered and I put him back on the snowboard. I took him back to the top of the slope and then we repeated what we did several times. By the time I was finally noticing that he was mastering it, I had to wipe the sweat off his forehead. "That was amazing," he said afterward, and I could only agree with him.

I took him out of the snowboard boots and then left the equipment where we had found it. I could see that he was wishing we didn't have to leave it behind, but we had that other thing I promised him we were going to do.

We were standing in front of it, and the smile on Mikey's face was as radiant as it had ever been. It was a somewhat big and not too tall Christmas tree that was going to be perfect for this Christmas.

And we were going to decorate it together.

CHAPTER 11

Slipping back into my old self was amazing, and I was happy I shared that moment with him. Chris was unlike any person I knew. He was caring, loving, and was showing me that I was ready for real love – and especially after we left here. The sun was already going up above the trees and we could feel that the temperatures were rising. Things were definitely getting better here.

We didn't have enough space for the Christmas tree inside the cabin, so we had to put it outside. I wasn't having the Christmas I thought I would when I came to this mountain, but it was still better than all the other Christmases I had before.

My Daddy was lifting me and I was putting a weird, different pine cone that we found lying around the cabin at the top of the tree. His hands were holding me tightly by my waist, and I felt so safe it didn't even cross my mind that I was a couple of feet above the ground.

I moved the cone and then pulled it down so that it was fixed at the top of the tree. Out of sheer luck, we managed to find some baubles and tinsels we put on the tree's branches.

Daddy lowered me until my feet were on the ground, sinking into the snow. I whirled around and hugged him tightly. I was feeling the heat of his body and the beating of his heart, and they were some of the best things about him.

"The only thing we are missing is some gifts, but I promise that when we get out of here, I'm going to buy you many. I don't have a lot of money, but I have enough for that."

The prospect of him giving me some gifts was thrilling. I couldn't wait until I was walking down the stairs in my house and finding, under the tree, his gifts. "Yes, Daddy! I can't wait for that."

I turned around again, this time taking in the Christmas tree that was in front of us. The sun was behind us and it was so bright that it was highlighting all the details of the tree. It was really beautiful, especially with the baubles and tinsels we covered it with.

He grabbed my hand and took me back inside the cabin. Pushing the door, he could barely close it. We didn't have much to do right now other than to wait for dinner time, which was something I was excited about.

He sat on the bed and I sat there with him. His hand was big and comforting like always, and I had a very important thing to tell him right now. I was looking into his eyes when I said, "You are the most amazing person I've met in the world. I want you to know that. You are a biker and it's so surprising to me that you are like this. I really meant it when I said I don't like people like you."

Chris put his hand on my cheek and caressed it. "You know, there's something you said to me when I first met you and, if you don't mind, I'd like you to tell me about it this time."

"What do you mean? I don't follow you."

"You said that a biker ruined your life, and you didn't elaborate. I want to know why, and I want to know who the biker was. Not saying that I'm going to go after him, just that I think we should clear that up."

I looked down, realizing that he wasn't going to drop this issue. Now that we were talking about it, I wasn't feeling like being his Little anymore right now. Not at the moment, anyway. Maybe sometime later. But right now, he was bringing back memories I thought I had forgotten a long time ago.

"There was this biker called Jean who was really close to me. He knew my father and was one of his friends. One of his best friends, I should say. He was a nice guy who knew that I was gay. We got pretty close and I thought we were becoming the couple I had always dreamed about."

Chris squeezed my hand slightly. "Go on. I'm here to give you all the support you need."

I felt a tear coming out and rolling down my cheek. It had been such a dark moment in my life I didn't want to remember anything about it. "We were kind of having some dates and going out often, and that was before I told everyone I was gay. He got pretty mad that I was hiding from doing that and pretending that it wasn't something I needed to do, and then he thought he had enough of it. I thought he was just going to break up with me, but then he decided to tell everyone about my secret. I was still finding out who I was, and I was pretty stressed out when my father came telling me he knew about it. I thought that he was going to stop paying for my college."

I was trying to hold back the tears, but now they were coming out in full force. My eyes were bawling out and I was sobbing. Chris put his arm around me and pulled me to him. He was hugging me as he bathed me with his warmth. I couldn't be doing this without him. And then I decided to tell him something I thought I was going to hold back until the time was right.

"We were really close and I never thought he was just going to betray me like that. We didn't even kiss, but I was in love with him. I fell in love with him too quickly, just like it's happening now with you."

Chris was still hugging me tightly, and being in his arms was very comforting. I'd be thinking about killing myself right now if he wasn't here.

"Thank you for telling me that. I don't know who that guy was, but he was an asshole, and he never deserved you. You didn't deserve him, and I can promise you that things are going to be different with me. I'm going to treat you with the respect and love you need."

I turned my head to look at him, my lips approaching his and then connecting. I was finally having my first kiss, and it was everything I thought it was going to be. His lips were very sweet, tender, and soft. I could be kissing them for hours on end if it was possible.

There was no tongue going into my mouth, which was something I appreciated. I felt uncomfortable, awkward, and like I was going to ruin this. After all, this being my first kiss, I had no idea what I was doing.

A moment later, Chris retreated his head as he looked deeply into my eyes. "So how was that for your first kiss?"

I blinked twice. It was difficult to process exactly what happened and what was still happening. This was turning into the trip of my life. One moment I was finding out everything about the man that wanted to become my boyfriend and the next I was kissing him.

"It was amazing. Could we do it again?" I asked, and then he put his hand on my cheek again and caressed it.

"Of course. Whatever you want," he answered and kissed me while pushing me against the wall of the cabin. He was being gentle and forceful at the same time, and I was accepting every part of it. My hands were going under his shirt and coat, and was pulling them both up. I wanted to see what was hiding under them. I wanted to see what he was like without them on.

And things were getting so heated up between us that I was almost forgetting we were in a cabin, a storm raging outside. It took me a try, but I was finally taking off his coat and shirt, my eyes taking a while to process what I was seeing.

His chest was just perfect, lines delineating his muscles, and shadows where they should be. They moved as he breathed slowly, and I could feel the lust that was consuming his mind.

"I don't have a condom, but that's okay. There are plenty of other things we can do without it." He took a deep breath in. "But before that, I need to know if you're ready for this."

I wasn't going to say anything so I just nodded. He smiled gently and then pulled me up with his strong, confident arms. Chris started to pepper my neck with several kisses that were driving me nuts. I was squirming underneath him, and this was everything I thought it was going to be.

I was just hoping that in a couple of days from now we could leave the mountain and I could take him to my house. When we got there, we would have all the privacy and time we needed.

CHAPTER 12

Chris

I was lying in his bed next to Mike, his hand resting on my chest as he showed me how much he trusted me. My hand was on his back and I was caressing it gently. His skin was very smooth and soft, like cotton. I could be doing this for hours on end if he wasn't already waking up.

I looked outside and opened a gentle smile when I remembered that we weren't on the mountain anymore. I was at his home and it was big and spacious. His friends and some cops found us in the cabin when most of the snow melted. I even found my bike again and I was still toying with the idea of teaching Mike how to ride it. He was way more worried about his college stuff, so I still hadn't had the opportunity to do that, though.

He cracked open his eyes, looking at me and showing me that, right now, he was an adult in his mind and also my boyfriend. His hand was going down, moving over my belly, and he was now grabbing my cock. I was already hard before he did that, and now I was much harder. He stroked at the skin gently, and I was drooling so much I was pretty sure that soon pre-come was going to be coming out of the slit.

"I love you so much," he murmured, his other hand caressing my belly and showing me how much he loved my abs. And it wasn't just that his skin was very soft, but also that it was warm and was inviting me to do things with him I never thought possible.

I moved my head until I was kissing his forehead. "I love you too," and saying that felt right. After all the misguided relationships I had, I was finally having one where I felt I was in control and was with the right person.

My hand went for the dresser which was by the bed. I opened a drawer and fished out a condom package. I ripped it open with a hand and my teeth, saying, "At least this time I'm ready for it. We can do it, if you want."

I was living a dream. Sleeping with my boyfriend, waking up to him in my arms, and smelling how great he smelled in the mornings. I wanted to take his virginity, but only if he was willing.

He blinked once and smiled gently. He was smiling without showing his teeth, and that was everything I thought I needed to take things up a notch.

Moving my hand down, I found his ass and squeezed it. I was squeezing it with enough force to show that I was in control of everything. He could give himself fully to me and I was going to make sure that he was going to have an amazing time with me.

"Put it in your mouth," I asked of him slowly, my voice a little throaty. "Show me what you can do with it."

He positioned himself so that his mouth was right above my cock. Taking a deep breath in, he closed his eyes as he took in what they were seeing. He was enjoying this, and I could tell how much this moment meant to him.

It was no wonder that his shaft was hard and he was leaking pre-come. Seeing that, I reached out with my hand and grabbed his balls. They weren't as big as mine, but they were still his balls. I squeezed and played with them gently, loving the littles moans escaping his mouth. He wanted me now as much as I wanted him.

"Make me come, baby. Make me come," I mumbled, closing my eyes and feeling as he pushed up more of my cock into his mouth. I thought that Mike was going to be a little shy about it, but he was showing me the opposite. His hands were gliding over my athletic body, and he was pressing his fingers into it every time he wanted. He was doing that skillfully, and I didn't think he had it in him.

Since we made out in the cabin and I sucked him off, he was showing so much more of him.

Mike was swirling his tongue around my mushroom head and was making wet sounds that were kicking me over the moon. My body was getting hotter and hotter, and my balls were tensing up. I wasn't going to come right now, but what he was doing was making that so hard. I wanted to come inside his mouth and make it feel tacky and wetter than it was.

"I love you so much," I said, my hand going over his back and feeling his ass again. He was letting out more little moans as I squeezed his buttcheeks gently. I was even digging my fingers inside his asscrack and looking for his tight hole. I couldn't wait until I was inside him and fucking him gently. I couldn't wait until he was clenching his walls around me and knotting with me.

And I couldn't wait until, one day, we were doing this without a condom.

Picking up speed, he was bobbing up and down on my dick, and my balls were tensing up so much I thought I was already going to explode. But then he stopped for a moment, reopening his eyes and looking into my pupils. Mike was telling me that he was ready to take things to a new level, and I was more than willing to make that happen.

"Turn around," I murmured into his ear and he didn't just do that, but also got on his knees on the bed. I picked up the condom, put it on, and then grabbed him by his hips. I moved so that I was right behind his hole and then lined up my cock. I could see that he was trembling, and that reminded me that I needed to be careful with this.

I pushed my hips forward and then penetrated him, moving inside slowly. I was stretching his walls and he was groaning softly. I could see that Mike was shaking and that I needed to give him some time until he was used to my size.

Caressing his back gently, I asked, "Feeling okay right now? I can do this more slowly, if you want."

"No, I'm okay. Keep going, please," he said, his voice a little low but still with the same tone I was used to. Hearing what he said brought a smile to my face, and I didn't waste time as I started to move in and out of him. Mike was incredibly tight, and I was stretching his walls like this was his destiny. He was still moaning softly and showing me how much he wanted this, and I was just happy that I was making it all happen for him.

I picked up my pace when I felt that he was better used to my size. Mike was still hard and leaking pre-come. He couldn't hide the orgasm that was slowly taking over his body. His balls were getting smaller and I was pretty sure that he was close to blowing his load over the bed.

He let out a long, raspy moan when he came with me. He was shooting his load all over the bedsheets and his body was shaking much more than before. It was so hot inside of him it was difficult for me to extend this much more than it was already lasting.

I started to blow my load inside the condom as I felt all the tension that was in my body seeping out. I stopped fucking him and stayed still while my orgasm was still happening. My hands were grabbing his waist and I was finding it pretty slippery. He was sweating quite a bit and I could hear his panting.

Mike had a smile on his face, showing me that he thought that it was all worth it. His legs were still trembling even a minute after the end of our fuck. I was resistant to pulling out of him, and I wanted him to remember my size. He needed to do that because we were certainly going to be doing this many more times in the future.

We both flopped down on the bed and I pulled him until I was hugging him tightly. Looking into his eyes and then kissing his lips briefly, I asked, "So, how was that for a first time? There's a lot more where that came from."

He kissed me back, saying, "It was amazing and I can't wait to do it again with you."

But before that, there was something else I wanted to do with him.

MIKE'S EPILOGUE

He pulled me out of the bathtub, holding me in his arms gently. He kissed my forehead and even though I was naked, never before did I feel so safe with someone. That was the whole meaning behind finding my other half. He was the person I felt the safest with.

He put me back on the floor and even though there was a rug under my feet, it was still a little slippery. I didn't feel that I was going to fall over because he was the one holding me, his hands under my armpits. And the gentle smile on his face was as relieving as the warmth of his body.

"Whoa there, sunshine. You need to be a little more careful when stepping out of the bathtub." And as he finished saying that, he rubbed my hair vigorously.

"How can I do that when you make me feel so safe all the time? I feel like I can always be myself whenever you are with me."

Chris didn't have a shirt on, instead opting to have just his boxers on. He wasn't hard, though. This was just a sweet moment that he was sharing with me, and once he finished toweling me dry, he'd change my diaper. I couldn't wait until he was doing that.

And as soon as I thought that, he grabbed a towel, looped it around me, and started rubbing it over my body. First, over my legs, then my groin, my ass, and my back, and the rest of my body. He pulled it up and then started to rub it on my hair, drying it.

But seeing that my hair was still wet, he decided to pick up the hair dryer and blow it at my head. He rubbed it gently with his fingers as he kept the device pointed at it. Chris only stopped when he noticed that my hair couldn't get any dryer than it already was.

"There, that should do it. As dry as it can get," he said, widening his smile slightly.

"Yes, Daddy!" I said, jumping out of the bathroom and then flopping down on the bed. We didn't have a changing table big enough for me yet, but I was planning on buying one. In the meantime, we could keep using the bed every time I needed my diaper changed. This time, it was going to be my first time having my diaper changed, and it was going to be incredible.

Chris was also changing his life for the better. He found work at a multinational company as a bodyguard, and that meant he was dropping his biker life for good. That was great, I thought. It meant that he was always going to be living with me and that he was never going to be worried again the cops might lock him up.

Chris was chuckling as he came back into the room, grabbing all the things he was going to need from the drawer. A bottle of skin cream, talcum, and a large diaper that was the right size for me. "No need to hurry things up, little one. We've got all the time we need."

I nodded frantically. I knew we had, but I was still impatient about someone putting a diaper on me for the first time. This whole time, I knew I was a little, but I never dared to put a diaper on by myself. It just didn't feel right.

I had a king-sized bed and I could lie down on one side of it, and he could use the other one to spread the diaper. That's what he did, moving his hand to ask me to put myself on it. When my butt was on the material of the diaper, I was already giggling. I was feeling like I wasn't my normal self anymore. Or rather, I should be saying that I was finally feeling like who I had always been.

"This is your first time having someone put a diaper on you, and I want to make it special," Chris said, pulling up the sides of the diaper and then connecting them after applying the talcum and the skin cream. Feeling the diaper on me was making me feel so comfortable with myself and everything going on in my life.

That was fast, but it was expected coming from someone that had changed so many diapers in his life. Chris patted the front of the diaper and then lied down on the bed. Propping his head on his hand, he was looking into my eyes and I knew he had something important to tell me. I couldn't wait until he was saying the words.

"I love you so much that I want to teach you how to ride a bike. I want to travel with you all over the country and I know you are thinking the same thing." He took a deep breath in, smelling how nice I smelled. "What do you say? Interested?"

Hearing what he was proposing made my heart jump. It was everything I wanted since leaving that mountain. "Do I even need to answer? Of course I want to do that, Daddy!" And this time, I didn't even have to change my voice to sound more like the Little I was. It just came naturally to me.

"And then, we could start thinking about telling everyone you know about the fact you are a Little and that I'm your daddy."

I pursed my lips. Telling my parents – and especially my father – would be difficult. Even though he was understanding of what was happening with me when I told him I was gay, saying to him that I was a little was a different matter entirely.

Still, I could tell that it was worth it.

CHRIS' EPILOGUE

"Come on, there's nothing scary about it. It's just a bike, like all the others." That's what I was saying to him, but it wasn't changing the way he was looking at it. Mike just wasn't used to riding motorcycles, and I could see why it was that way. His whole life, he had always been the kind of person that would work in an office and come back home in his car.

But riding a motorcycle was an entirely different beast. He needed to shift the gears and pay more attention to the road than he would when driving his car.

He turned around quickly, smiling from ear to ear. "Can't we do again what we did before, you riding the bike and I sitting behind you?"

I rubbed his hair vigorously. That hadn't been the first time we did it, and he really said he wanted to learn how to ride my motorcycle. I was a little disappointed that he was already chickening out on it, though.

"Alright," I said, giving in. "We are going to do that again, but only because you asked nicely. When we come home, I'm going to give you something nice. A gift for your good behavior."

"Yes, Daddy!" He said, jumping several times in a row. I put a hand on his shoulder and stopped that. I didn't want him potentially falling over and getting hurt. "I can't wait to ride to New York with you."

I grabbed his hand, got on my bike, and put him behind me. Mike wrapped his arms around me and held onto me tightly. He positioned his head in the crook of my neck and I didn't do anything while he listened to the beating of my heart. It was his way of telling me he was feeling a little anxious and just needed to listen to it to feel better.

When he stirred up a little, I twisted the handlebars as I turned on the motorcycle. The engine roared up to life, and I could feel his body shaking behind me.

"She has a nasty bite, but I'm sure she won't bite you – as long as I'm around," I said, turning my head around so that I was looking into his beautiful eyes and seeing exactly what he was thinking.

"Then, whenever I am around her, I am going to make sure you are with me."

I chuckled. "I'm sure you're going to. You are so scared of her it's kind of funny."

I twisted the handlebars again, propelling the bike forward as we entered the road. Feeling the wind blowing against my face was already washing away all the anxiety I had.

I felt his hand pressing against my chest and I knew he had something he wanted to tell me. "I'm actually changing my mind about wanting to learn how to ride this motorcycle. If you don't mind, I don't think I want to try again."

He had his helmet on, but I didn't. I was pretty confident about my skills when on a bike, and I loved feeling the wind blowing against my face.

I arched my eyebrows. "Really? That's a little disappointing, but okay. I want you to always feel safe with me, and if there's one thing I want to promise you is that I'll never force anything on you."

"I'm so glad you understand me."

He was hurting my heart a little, but that was okay. Every relationship had some speed bumps, and that was a tiny little one.

Turning my head back so that I was focusing on the road, I said as I raised my voice to be heard in the wind, "Don't worry. Just focus on enjoying the trip because it's going to take a long time to get there. But I'm sure that when you are seeing Manhattan in the distance, you are going to be pleased we are doing this."

And so I rode away with Chris on my bike and I knew that our lives were going to be perfect together.

I found my other half.

The End

Thank you for reading the story! If you're looking for the first two books of this series, check them out here:

1. Rockstar's Little: ABDL MM Halloween Romance

2. Doctor's Little: ABDL MM Halloween Romance

Lastly, leave a review for this book if you liked it. It really helps us a lot!

ROCKSTAR'S LITTLE

ABDL MM HALLOWEEN ROMANCE

Max

I was in my room, leaning over my table. In front of me, my notebook, sheets of paper, and my computer. On the other side of the room, scratches on the wall. My cat was curled up on herself, sleeping and snoring. Sweat was pooling on my forehead and I could only wonder when I was going to finish my homework.

My hand was holding a pencil, and I hated calculus. I kept wondering why we had to keep trying to solve these problems. It wasn't like I'd use them when I was working for a company, right?

A notification popped up on the screen of my computer and my hands flew to the keyboard. It was my friend, saying that he also couldn't find solutions to the problems. I smiled, knowing that was one of the few things still making me happy tonight.

It was so good to know Claude always had my back.

Me: I know, right? I also don't know the answer to problem one.

Claude: It's going to get better, I'm sure of it. You just need to believe in yourself.

Believing in myself was one of the things I thought I'd never be able to master. It was so hard. Dating? Forget that. It was impossible for someone like me to date, especially at a college that was so conservative.

It was like I could feel people judging me all the time. Eyes on me, always checking out what I was doing. I was gay and I couldn't even go to a bar without checking out the guys there. They were all my type. Well, most of them were anyway.

And I had no idea why my mind was even thinking about that sort of thing right now. I knew it was kind of impossible, but I still tried to control those thoughts. I just wanted to have one night where I didn't have to think about those things. One night when I was alone and all I had was my homework.

I looked at the screen of the computer again and noticed that my friend had gone offline. It was just like him to disappear from time to time. To be honest, that was what I should be doing right now. I should be focusing on myself and my homework.

I looked outside, happy that at least I was living in my own apartment. It was solitary, but noises were absent. I could even sleep now and I was feeling pretty sleepy.

The only thing keeping me from sleeping was my homework. Seeing all of the sheets of paper on the table, my notebook, my laptop computer, and my pencil and eraser was driving me nuts.

I took a deep breath and tried to control my thoughts. The last thing I wanted now was to fall into another spiral of depression. I had depression once and I could never have it again. I almost killed myself then.

It was thanks to my only friend that that didn't happen. And he knew that, which made me pretty sure he was going to talk to me again soon. Part of my mind was begging for him to do that.

I took another look around the room and noticed posters on the walls. I was a pretty big fan of a rock band and I was dying on the inside to go see them when they came here. It was going to happen next week. I invited my friend to go there with me and he said he was going to. I liked going with him to places, and even though he said he wasn't into the rock band much, he said he was going there with me anyway. Just to keep me company.

I sighed, worked on the homework a little more, and tried not to freak out about it. The last thing I needed now was freaking out about anything. Just wanted to remain calm and pretend I really was going to get that Economics degree.

I hated this college. Just wanted to get out of it as soon as possible and find a place that didn't despise me as much. It even had a church on campus, and I was forced to go to mass even though I didn't want to.

This whole thing was such a mess.

A notification popped up on the screen again.

Claude: Something's on TV. I think you should turn it on.

Me: And you're not even going to tell me what it is?

Claude: Not this time :)

I sighed, standing up. I was happy I didn't have to keep trying to finish that homework. And the due date? It was tomorrow morning, or maybe today. I didn't know for sure. I wasn't keeping track of time anymore. Doing that made me feel nervous and I hated that.

When I stood up, my cat cracked open her eyes. A collar was around her neck, with her name engraved on a small pin. Chill. It also had a tracker and some other things in case she disappeared.

I lived in an apartment and I'd never let her out without my permission. It was something we established when I found her. She'd been lost in an alleyway and I couldn't have let her there all by herself. Still had no idea who dumped her there, though. And I didn't think I'd ever find out.

I walked up to her, got on one knee, and she purred as I rubbed her head. Her fur was just so soft and gentle. I could keep rubbing it for hours on end…

Blake

I pushed past the people in front of me, unhappy that they were standing in my way. Didn't they know I was going to sing? And I wasn't just going to do that. I was going to rock the audience and make them think I was the best rockstar in the world.

Sweat pooled on my forehead and in my armpits. It wasn't the first time I was going to sing in front of so many people, and instead of that making me feel afraid, it energized me.

Nothing better than giving thousands of people what they came here for.

I dashed through the curtains, the roar of the crowd erupting at the same moment. I smiled, checking out the stadium. All I could see was the forest of dancing people, and the flashlights of their phones.

I was holding my electric guitar, my colleagues already positioned with their instruments. They were going to help me play the song or the collection of songs that I was going to master.

Couldn't wait until-

And ah, there it was. The crowd erupted again when the stage lights focused on me. Cocaine was one hell of a drug, and I couldn't be doing this without it.

I was addicted to it. I knew I should do something about it, but the truth of the matter was that I couldn't feel like this without first taking some hits. It's why I always felt overconfident.

Without it, intrusive thoughts started to creep into my mind, and I couldn't have that.

My fingers moving against the strings, I start to sing and shake my head, my long and blonde hair flying with me. The crowd roared again, their phones shining their flashlights.

It was dark. The moon was just above the walls of the stadium, making the place feel even more alive than it was.

And it wasn't just my fingers and head that were moving frenetically, but also my body. I couldn't stay still for a second, dashing from left to right and vice-versa, thinking about nothing but my song.

My clothes were tight. Rockstars like myself were few and far between these days, but that was okay. I had a bigger audience and more people sucking up to me than usual, I thought with a smile.

And the crowd erupted again, my ears and eyes noticing the front rows. They weren't just singing with me, but they were also chanting my name and that was a lot more than I thought I'd ever achieve in my life when I was little. Just never thought I'd have so much fame one day and that I'd be dealing so well with it.

For a moment, my eyes landed on something. Nothing more than a shadow of something that couldn't have anything to do with me, right? Wrong. The moment my eyes found it, I already froze up and couldn't focus on the song anymore.

Goddamnit, I couldn't fail now. If I looked like a fool in front of all these people, I'd lose all my sponsorships and everyone around the globe would think I was a scam.

But what I saw… It was no mistake. She was there. The woman I thought I'd marry one day.

And my eyes also noticed someone else. A man who appeared to be as young as 18 years old, standing in the middle of the crowd, too far from the front rows. I shouldn't have noticed him and yet he was now the only thought in my mind, other than my ex.

I went on, rocking and singing, shaking my head and scrubbing the strings of the guitar with my fingers. Breathing more rapidly and sweating even more than before, I was already happy the show was ending.

Couldn't get her out of my head and couldn't stop thinking about that guy. Time for the contest's result, I remembered.

I slid across the floor, sweeping my hands one last time over the strings of the guitar and closing my eyes. A huge explosion of fireworks in front of me and the crowd roared once more.

I had a rose in my mouth. Shooting up, I tossed it to the crowd and turned around. Everyone chanted my name and my band clapped, thanking me for another spectacular performance.

I walked through the curtains and into the changing room, falling into the chair. Hairdressers and other employees surrounded me, fixing me up.

"The contest's result, sir. They're here," someone said and I perked up. Ahhh, the contest, of course. I was supposed to talk to some fans after the show tonight and I thought it would be cool if we gave everyone a fair chance.

After some last makeup retouches, I made the chair whirl around and shot up, saying, "Let them in. I'm ready."

Camera men stormed into the room, ready to record the conversation I was going to have with my fans. I felt excited, but not nervous. Talking with my fans was one of the good things about being famous.

Someone opened the door and they stepped in. I froze up for a moment, realizing that one of the guys was the same I'd spotted in the crowd. Either God existed, or someone was playing a trick on me. Of all the people I could have singled out, he was one of the winners of the contest? Really?

ABDL MM SERIES AND MORE

SERIES - SWEET PACIS

1. My Caring Biker: An ABDL MM Biker Romance

2. My Loving Biker: An ABDL MM Biker Romance

3. My Protective Biker: An ABDL MM Biker Romance

4. My Obsessive Biker: An ABDL MM Biker Romance

5. My Possessive Biker: An ABDL MM Biker Romance

SERIES - NOT ENOUGH DIAPERS

1. Be my ABDL: A Gay Age Play Romance
2. Regressing the Rookie: A Gay Age Play Romance
3. Regressing the Recruit: An ABDL Romance

SERIES – REGRESSED

1. Gifting Crayons: An ABDL MM Romance
2. Sugar Mister: An ABDL MM Romance
3. Loving Little Chris: An ABDL MM Romance
4. Bedtime for Cody: An ABDL MM Romance
5. Little Crayons: An ABDL MM Romance

Or, if you'd like, you can download this collection instead to have all of those stories together:

Fussy Littles: An ABDL MM Romance Bundle

Gay first time romances:

One Kiss Less: A Sci-Fi MM Romance
No Turning Back: A Gay Arranged Marriage Romance
Just Say Yes: An Arranged Marriage M/M Romance

Or everything in a convenient box-set:

Against All Odds: A Gay Romance Bundle

ABOUT THE AUTHORS

Jerry Hastings

Jerry Hastings is a passionate gamer, an outspoken lover of his PS4, an advocate for minority rights, and a staunch supporter of the fight against homophobia. Much more than putting words on paper, his stories change people's lives and minds.

As a writer, his specialty is gay romance. His tales are spicier and more affectionate than those usually found elsewhere. Have your soothing tea ready, because his words will make your heart beat faster than it should.

Michael Levi

Michael Levi's biggest passion? Writing steamy, romantic stories that leave his readers panting. He's currently focusing on ABDL MM romances, but his collection is diverse and there are books for everyone's tastes. If you're looking for straight to gay, first time, BBC, sissification, and more, you're going to find them on his author page.

He lives to pamper his readers, every kiss means a lot more than what meets the eye, and he loves his Alpha males. Making sure that every gay first time feels different, Michael Levi writes his stories with a cup of coffee by his side. And for inspiration, he always opens up a photo of his new crush.

9 798777 091710